THE BIG RED BUCKLE

THE BIG RED BUCKLE

MATTHEW ALAN THYER

FEETFORBRAINS PUBLISHING

Published by FeetForBrains Publishing

ISBN-13: 978-0615934167
ISBN-10: 0615934161

Typesetting services by BOOKOW.COM

to Tess, The most romantic thing we've ever done was read books together.

Acknowledgements

Tess Thyer, Thomas Thyer, Matthew Amend, and Eric Beckendorf. I could not have done this without you entertaining my wild imagination. You guys are the best.

Also, my sincere thanks go out to all those helpful writers and friends at LittleSpec. I really appreciate all the input I got from this quarter and wish I could still be making weekly pilgrimages to talk shop with you all.

Finally, to all the excellent women at North Boulder Recreation Center that watched my little one while I was banging away at my computer. You guys are the best.

Epigraph

More than anything else the sensation is one of perfect peace mingled with an excitement that strains every nerve to the utmost, if you can conceive of such a combination.

— Wilbur Wright

CONTENTS

STARTING LINE

The back of the pack is where Marco lines up. Most of the racers jostle for position at the edge of the starting line, elbows out or lightweight carbon trekking poles spread in an effort to secure that little extra advantage. Race favorites like Gregory Neal and Franz Wickenhauser are on the line pushing shoulders and helmets against one another, more for the cameras than anything else. It will not matter.

Each of them has around 1500 kilometers of The Race extending from their place at the starting line across an equatorial wilderness and up two massive volcanoes. Officially titled 'The Grand Martian Traverse,' the course starts at the base of Ascraeus Mons and finishes in the cloud city of Buena Suerte atop Olympus Mons. Perhaps more popular on Earth than in the colonies, The Race draws the sport's most elite endurance athletes and massive crowds. As well as sponsorship and money, it is where you need to be if you want to get made in the sport of endurance soaring.

Marco Aguilar has a few local sponsors, but only just enough to afford the new wing and harness packed on his back. The ultra-light life support suit and air scrubber he wears came out of his budget. It is all new gear, and largely untested, crafted here on Mars. Nothing like the fancy suits and wings the top competitors use. They can afford to scratch their visors on Day One because a stack of reserve helmets await them in fleets of support vehicles just a little way up the hill.

Marco tries to calm his mind and concentrate on the race immediately ahead of him. The climb up Ascraeus is about 15,000 meters from the starting line to the first major turn near the summit. Most of the racers will run to the northeastern side of the shield volcano, traversing on foot more than climbing, then deploy their wings to thermal up the mountain. The village of Tharsis is located on the cool, south side of the mountain, giving the obvious advantage to those who can reach the early morning sunlight first and begin soaring quickly. Flying is always faster than running.

For Marco, just being near the starting line right now represents the culmination of two years of careful preparation and training. He feels a momentary pang of guilt knowing that Emma has carried their family while his focus has been elsewhere. But he also knows that winning the GMT is a shared decision, not just his goal. Just like living part-time in the micro-settlement and the rest of the time in the rover, they both get something out of this attempt. For her, maybe more than for himself, it is the opportunity to sever a bad relationship with Earth just that much more. Emma feels the Earth's influence more keenly than Marco ever will, and it makes her skin crawl every time she is confronted with evidence of how they change things here on Mars. She wants Mars to stand on its own, let the colonies grow without the influence of Earth or its muddy history. Marco harbors no such great resentment for Earth. He simply loves to soar. But now, with the elbow of a visiting Earthling jabbing him in his side, he can understand her animus.

Marco sees his wife standing behind a throng of media and race fans on the side of the road. Emma lifts their baby, Grace, over her head and onto her slim shoulders so that both of them can make out his green suit and orange pack in the mass of racers. Marco waves and puts his hand to his face mask to blow a kiss in their direction. Then, in his ear a race official's warning, there are only seconds until the start. "Racers are reminded to head to their designated airlock at the Robinson Street junction."

Having a low overall ranking in the elite racer class saddles Marco with another disadvantage. His group will exit the southern airlocks near the town's main entrance, then run around the outside of the city. The highly ranked will head out as a set in the northeastern sector of the buried city with far less distance to negotiate. Even had he sponsors and money, Marco knows that he could never qualify for the top tier. He is a Martian and could not remain competitive soaring or racing on Earth, where most of the qualifying races are held, and where the gravity is so much stronger. Marco takes several deep breaths listening to the countdown, attempting to calm his heart and mind.

A loud beep is transmitted through his visor glass and the mass of racers surges into the lighted city streets. The leaders at the front of the line are sure to be sprinting with the media hover cams following overhead. Packed into the narrow street behind, Marco and the other racers can only manage to slowly shuffle forward.

He trots along, feeling the press of the race around him, and forces himself to stick to his planning. The pace slowly picks up. Soon the mass of racers spill into Robinson Street junction, a roundabout near the center of town, pushing against one another like flotsam at the leading edge of a flash flood. Marco peels away from the mob after running with them around three-quarters of the circular road. Other racers exit via one of five assigned routes, heading to their designated air locks. Now Marco opens up and starts moving fast along the mostly deserted route. He has trained hard for this part of the race, and knows he will soon be able to gain an advantage. But in the tiny mirrors set into the edge of his helmet, Marco notices someone flanking him in a lime green and white race suit. Further back other racers follow, but this guy holds tight to his heel.

Marco's route winds through the town heading first west, then south. Once the race exits the city, his path will be open and completely up to him. The heads-up display inside his helmet illuminates his route, indicating he is near the airlock. Six aero-fans support a hover camera, its lens trained on him, floating a couple of meters ahead and matching his pace. Marco begins to pour on the speed hoping to clear the airlock ahead of the rest of the racers keeping pace with him. He wonders momentarily if the floating camera caught the change in pace, but then as his body's oxygen debt rises, he reflexively returns his attention to his breath.

At the inside hatch of the airlock, he punches the open button and steps into the chamber. His lungs are burning with the effort to stay ahead of the pack. As he turns to shut the door, the green suited figure steps through the portal with him. Marco winces, but cycles the holding chamber despite its second occupant.

TRAVERSE

"As anticipated, Wickenhauser and Neal are battling it out on the high trail. It's 6:32 on the morning of the first day of the Grand Martian Traverse, and the pack is already starting to spread out as the racers seek sunshine and lift. Even at this early stage of the race you can see how much the competitors desire that Big Red Buckle." The camera switches from an aerial shot of bobbing headlamps and silhouetted figures in the early dawn tundra of Ascraeus Mons to a pair of men seated behind a desk. "I'm Bill Vance," says the dark, trim-haired member of the pair, "and with me, for the duration of the GMT, is Toma Crysta. Toma is a three-time champion of The Race, and has some insight into what it takes, not just to survive, but to win this amazing journey. Toma, what can you tell us about what we're seeing this morning?"

The thin, shaggy haired man sitting next to Vance smiles and starts talking to the camera with a thick Slavic accent. "Bill, this year's race is good one. Wickenhauser of Team Advanced took early lead from starting line effectively shutting out slower starters. Greg Neal from Rebel Gliders was able to catch up after leaving airlocks. Many of elite racers are following Neal's pace hoping to reach Gaisburg launch site near the head of line. I anticipate many of them will try to pass on first soaring leg of race."

The camera switches back to an aerial view of the race. Five figures are now in full sunlight and spaced closely. The voice of Bill Vance broadcasts over the audio channel, "Toma, this year's race has some native Martians in it.

What kind of showing are you expecting from them?" Spectators and fans periodically cluster along the trail. The racers jog along. Fans wave their arms and reach gloved and suited hands out to cheer on their favorites. The camera catches one spectator, who has altered his environmental suit to resemble a red devil, running alongside Greg Neal. In his own red suit, Neal quickly and easily outpaces his fan.

"Bill, is big question for everyone. None of Martian teams are seated well, and most race enthusiasts expect that Earth's gravity advantage will be difficult to overcome. Earth-side training is critical component of winning. But now is a new generation of Mars kids who have never set foot on home world. I wonder what they can do?"

"That's right. Of the one hundred and ten teams in this year's GMT, seven of them are native to Mars. And Toma, I'm hearing that two of them have broken off from the main advance and have set out on their own course. There has been speculation that they're lost. What do you make of this?"

"Yes," the camera again switches to two partially illuminated figures running down a steep scree slope, arms flailing to stay upright with the speed and unsteady footing, "Is difficult to make out team colors, but I'm told this is Marco Aguilar from Ulysses Fossae Micro-Settlement and Petrus Mandel from Pavonis Universal. These two left Tharsis via the southern air lock. Instead of running back around city, they are now headed down the shield wall of Ascraeus. I'm not sure what they could be up to. I think race is going to leave them in dust."

The camera pans out from the two jumping figures as they descend independently and alone in the rising sunlight, long shadows chasing them down the hill. The camera switches back to Bill Vance, just catching a brief flicker of annoyance betrayed in his pose of neutrality. "Really, Toma? You don't think these Martians stand a chance? I'm curious to find out what they're up to. Aguilar is well known for his flying near Tharsis. He holds the Solar System foot- launched distance record. Toma, didn't you attempt to take it back in

Idaho and then later here on the Tharsis Fosse?" There is a little bit of venom in this question.

Crysta responds with nonchalance, "Yes, conditions were not conducive on subsequent attempts. But you know Aguilar is young and, perhaps, lucky. Yes?"

Bill Vance is looking back into the camera lens. "Well Toma, I'm looking forward to seeing what this lucky Martian can do. Since his 789-kilometer record setting flight in 2108, we haven't heard much from Marco Aguilar. But as a Martian myself, I can tell you that we've been waiting to see what he's going to pull out of his sleeve next. He's a wild card in this race that many natives believe might be able to take the podium."

BREAKAWAY

Marco wants to lose this guy in the green and white. Every time he looks in his helmet mirror, he sees that big logo for Pavonis Universal right behind him. He looks again then growls inside his helmet, and feels someone tap him on his shoulder. Marco stops and turns. "What?" he yells inside his helmet.

The figure in the green suit points to the control pad on his wrist indicating that Marco should dial in to a particular radio frequency. Marco turns and, while jogging, switches his radio to the suggested channel.

"Why are you following me?" Marco barks into his radio. "Who are you?"

The voice that answers is labored. Marco thinks he's got this guy beat if he ever has to climb. "I'm Pet Mandel. Look, I know you've got a plan." He pants into the radio. "I know you run and fly here all the time. Dude, I read your posts on the net. Why the hell are we going down?" His words match the cadence of his breathing. "Where's the lift?"

Marco sighs inwardly. There is no chance to lose this guy on a descent. He will find out soon enough. "Have you ever done a flat-land launch?" The silence on the radio tells him that the answer to this question is no. He continues with an explanation, "If you can scratch, you can do this. Thermals won't start popping up at Gaisburg until the sun is really warm on the mountain. The air is just too thin for them to be meaningful this early in the morning and that high up."

Marco pauses for some deep breathing as he vaults down several large rocks. "There are a bunch of higher pressure breakpoints and thermal release sites lower down near the plains." His pace is settled enough that he can talk and run. "If you know what to look for, you can kite your wing until one of them picks you up and starts you soaring." Then it occurs to him that this guy is from the University. "Where did you learn to fly?"

"Umm, started with Nate Phillips at Pavonis."

That says it all, this kid might be following Marco into a death trap if that's all he's got. "Started with?"

"Yeah, he was an asshole." Pet takes a moment to breathe. "Dude was always fighting with his students." Breath. "Other instructors too. So after I got rated, I went on my own." His breathing starts to match the pace. "Been soaring for, what? Three years now." Pet is quiet while he steps over some volcanic ejecta. "Wish I could get my money back from him."

"Yes, I imagine." Marco commiserates with this tale of woe. It is not the first time he has heard those words from one of Phillips' students. "So you started flying on your own?"

"Oh yeah, got in way over my head too." Breath. "Sometimes at least, but there is a good group of guys." Breath. "Around Pavonis so I guess I had some help."

Pet's further explanation mollifies Marco's concerns somewhat. He decides that this kid can come along as long as he is able to keep up. "Listen, there's going to be some difficult flying today. I'll do what I can to help, but you're going to have to fly it on your own."

"Got it!" the response comes back. Pet recalls that they are still headed down the face of the volcano and not across the traverse. "By 'scratch' this low, do you mean trying to fly in zero lift until something pops?"

"Yes."

"I can do that, love to play on the cliff overlook in the Pavonis cone all the time. Wingovers in the setting sun after class."

Marco notices a hovercam off in the distance. The little robot momentarily eclipses the sun low on the eastern horizon. "Smile, you're on camera," he says. Adding, "If you can pull this off, you'll make history."

"Dude, I know, that's why I'm following you. To make history." He pauses mid-thought to breathe. Then, almost absentmindedly, "We're Martians, we do things together."

Marco chuckles at the slogan, "Sure, just don't hold me up."

Fifteen minutes later, Marco stops atop a little volcanic scarp about thirty meters high at the edge of the gradually sloping plane that extends out toward Poynting crater. He has since lost track of the hovercam, but imagines it is still there, waiting to see what might happen next. Pet silently unshoulders his wing and harness as soon as Marco starts to unpack. It is nearly 7:00 in the morning. They've been racing for a mere three hours and the main pack will still be plodding toward the Gaisburg launch for hours to come. There will not be a weasel fart of a thermal up there until 10:00, and that is only if they are lucky.

Marco tries to focus on routine. He moves to his pre-flight safety checks, starting with his suit. Despite decades of Terra-forming, Martian air is still too toxic to breathe. Thus Mars demands environmental suits for just about anything outside a pressurized and purified space. Marco wears a Martian redesign of the standard photobioreactor concept from Earth. It pulls the chilly, toxic soup from outside and turns it into something he can breathe using an embedded engineered microorganism, the light of the sun, and his movement. There is an auxiliary air tank located near the base of his spine, but it supplies only a couple of hours of air on the surface and it is for emergencies. He needs sunlight or his own movement to keep breathing. Compared to the Earth suits out there, which are powered by batteries and only augmented by solar input, this Martian design will allow him to go much further without support.

He starts at his feet, checking for punctures and abrasions and works his way up to where his visor makes it impossible to see himself. With the help of a small mirror on a retractable lanyard, he finishes his inspection. There is nothing to patch, nothing to worry him.

The wing comes out of its bag. Marco pulls the lines into a coil with long, deft arm movements until he has a pile that resembles a giant orange and green chrysanthemum of crisp technical fabric. The thin lines are laid down over the wing and he reverses the pack into a harness. He runs his eyes over the ultra-lightweight harness looking for anything that might make it less than flight worthy. The control surface for his suit and radio come off his left wrist and get snapped to the flight deck on the harness where he will be able to read them and manipulate them as necessary in the air. Next, he pulls shoulder straps over his suit and fastens leg straps and a waist belt. The wing lines come out of their coil and are attached to the harness.

Despite all this technology, on Mars, there is still no way to feel the wind blowing on your skin. Marco bends down and, with a gloved hand, picks up a bit of Martian soil then lets it sift through his fingers. He watches as the dust flows away and up the slope of Ascraeus Mons. He has the right location. Marco turns his back to the morning wind and extends the lines of his wing. In one movement, his body stiffens and his right arm guides the lines and wing above his head, inflating and then flying the paraglider. Marco turns to face into the wind and notices that Pet is not too far behind. With his wing flying overhead, Marco leans over his waist belt and takes three long, slow steps off the cliff.

His launch feels smooth and that lack of effort is what he strives for. He smiles at this. Soaring now, he sits back into the harness and glides back and forth in front of the scarp probing the air for anything that might take him up. Soon, Pet's white, gray, and green wing is following him along the scarp. The two fly back and forth a kilometer at a time in the ridge lift provided by the gentle and invisible flow of atmosphere over the scarp. They are waiting for the sun to heat a rock or barren patch of soil so that it will create a thermal column of air rising up the mountain.

Then, not ten minutes after they are both airborne, it happens. Marco enters the bubble first, his HUD registers the rise and his variometer begins to beep in his ear indicating the climb. He turns to the right, searching for the core of the thermal where the lift will be strongest. Pet sees Marco rise and directs his wing to this invisible spot knowing that he will enter the unseen elevator as well. Soon both men are circling tight at the core of the thermal.

Marco again notices the hovercam about 100 meters to their north. The robot drone is matching their altitude gain, but maintaining its distance. "Pet, right now there is a line of racers running up Ascraeus who are insanely jealous of you."

"Ho Marco, what do you mean?"

"That hovercam is still with us." Marco touches a couple of buttons on his control panel turning on the MBC broadcast of the race. The broadcast overlays Marco's view of the world outside his helmet. He sees the two of them circling ever higher along the southern steps of the volcanic shield, climbing meter by meter with rising air coming off the Martian plains far below.

"I see it, there. Yes, how high do you think this thermal is going to go?" Pet asks.

"I'd say we've got about half the climb before we need to transition. Be looking for your next trigger point. They'll all follow the high points along the mountain. We shouldn't have to go on glide for too long until we top out. Be ready for a rodeo ride. When we transition, the next one is going to be rough. They always are."

"I can handle a rough ride, it's the running I'm not looking forward to," responds Pet.

Marco has muted the MBC broadcast projected over his field of vision, he does not need the broadcast to know that at their current rate of climb they've just made the rest of the racers anxious and angry. Climbing at about 600 meters per minute, they will reach Gaisburg's elevation in about five minutes. It will take those runners almost seven hours of pain and exertion to reach that launch site. He chuckles to himself at this. What will appear to most a failed gambit will make up all the time they lost descending to the volcanic scarp launch, an intentional misdirection on Marco's part. Better, very shortly, they will have the barren plain above the town of Tharsis generating its usual and more powerful updraft, a big house thermal, that should rocket them to the first turn point of the race and well ahead of everyone running along the Gaisburg traverse.

Feeling a bit smug, Marco shuts down the MBC broadcast and focuses on turning and climbing as quickly as he can. He will be at the first turn point at noon while most of the rest of the racers will still be waiting for their turn to launch at Gaisburg.

SPEED

"Whoa, Neal and Wickenhauser are really pouring on the speed now. Look at them run. Do you imagine they've seen what the Martian teams are up to?" The screen shows two figures furiously making their way up the side of a mountain, arms pumping and legs kicking. The first face mask has a mirrored finish reflecting the sunlight, but as his head bobs in and out of the shot the face of the second runner can be seen gritting his teeth as he pushes his body to keep pace. The hover camera must be floating directly above the trail to get such a tight shot on them.

"Bill, you see look on Neal's face? He will not be giving up, not without fight." Crysta's voice is laid over the shot. "He has determination. And better Neal has Earth gravity at his core."

The camera switches to a computer generated image of the race, runners spread across the side of the volcano represented by little icons of running figures with their team colors below. There are two glider icons much higher up the mountain, approaching the cone atop Ascraeus.

Bill Vance's voice comes back over the audio channel. "It looked like Mandel and Aguilar were lost at first, but they've almost cleared the peak and the first turn point. What an upset! Teams along the Gaisburg traverse are scrambling to catch up." Just then, one of the runner icons along the traverse changes into a flyer somewhere near the middle of the main mass.

Crysta responds, "You must believe that support crews are looking at all options. In past, first ascent does not begin until much later in day. Once Mandel and Aguilar reach top of thermals, they have easy glide to second turn point at Sulci with hours of lead. Bill, in race like this, minutes of lead are difficult to overcome, but I know both Neal and Wickenhauser will chase down these young upstarts."

Bill Vance glances notices that teams are stopping as they run to Gaisburg and deploying their wings randomly and without any assurance that they will be able to fly. He interrupts Crysta's monologue. "Look, Toma. Racers are finding a place to deploy their wings anywhere along the trail. This Martian play has changed the program. No one knows what to do. What could happen now, Toma?"

The camera has moved from the animation to another aerial shot of several teams on the traverse dropping their rucksacks or in various stages of wing deployment along the trail. "They have seen two Martians pulling ahead and are making big gamble to find lift," Toma Crysta excitedly responds into his microphone. "They have no choice. Will there be lift? Who knows?"

To The Top

"We're going to ride this one to the top. Don't get out of the thermal at the cone," Marco says while fighting to keep the fist of air punching his wing hitting as close to the center as possible. "If we get off this elevator now all we'll find around it is sink."

Pet does not respond at once. He is fighting hard to ride the gnarly devil of rising air. Pet is maybe fifty meters below, flying in the punchy thermal. Without the experience Marco has accumulated, he must be fully engaged keeping his wing flying. Marco only hears grunts over the radio. He looks momentarily over his right shoulder and down. Sure enough, there is a white, gray and lime-green crescent below him standing out against the dull red of the Martian volcano like a rescue beacon. It is jerked sideways by what seems an invisible hand as the thermal grabs at Pet again.

Attempting to reassure, Marco says, "It's going to get better. Just don't think about grounding today. You're soaring, you're almost there."

Marco checks his lines again and glances at the altimeter display in his HUD. The inside tip of his wing has been collapsing periodically which is concerning. They have cleared the peak and are headed well over 25,000 meters already on this one. It is a squirrelly thermal that keeps hitting boundary layers. But it is also powerful enough to punch through each of these, just at weird angles, which is why the two of them are getting jerked around like puppets at the ends of very long strings. He knows this sort of flying is painful and dangerous, but with the first turn point behind them, they are still climbing and, soon, he is expecting to find a mountain wave.

With the thermal still jerking him around, Pet squeaks into his microphone, "Oh my god, oh my god. Shit, shit, shit!"

Marco hears the fear in his voice. Clearly, Pet has never flown in an equatorial dusty. "Take some deep breaths. Stay deep in the brakes. Try and center the lift as much as you can. You'll be okay." Marco takes his own advice.

"Never been … this high up." Pet stammers into his radio. "Damn it … this is hard."

Marco looks out at the horizon as he turns. The blackness of space is visible from this altitude. He can see stars as he rotates in the ever-rising air. Tharsis is not much more than a bare spot cooking in the sun far below as he circles. And there, just above, are the first signs of wave action.

As they rise, Marco makes out ice crystals forming a very thin lenticular cloud just above. These clouds are so thin and gossamer they cannot be seen from a distance. The thin layer of ice crystals flowing to the west marks the transition from the vertical flight they have struggled to achieve to enviable horizontal speed that will propel them across Ulysses Fosse and the vast desert separating them from Olympus Mons.

Marco radios down to Pet, "You're almost there. I can see the wave."

"What?" responds Pet. His disbelief obvious.

"We're going to surf the Ascraeus Mons mountain wave. It will be hard to see, but if you can feel it, you'll do fine. A lot like ridge soaring, but you don't want to bottom out or you'll get left behind."

"Seriously?" huffs Pet. "You lead, I'll follow." Marco can hear that things must be calming down for him too as the thermal slams into the jet-stream boundary layer and peters out beneath Pet's wing.

Marco's variometer only beeps intermittently now. This is the top of the climb. He points his glider west-northwest and steps on the speed bar, changing and steepening the angle of attack for his wing. Normally, this would just mean that he would move faster but descend faster too. In the wave, however, it is necessary to keep up with the air. He feels the acceleration and the wave picking him up.

"Stomp your bar once you get lined up for glide. Stomp it like it's going out of style," he radios to Pet.

"Gotcha, I've read about how this is done with sailplanes, but never done it myself."

Marco explains, "You've got to keep up with the wave. You're going to want to stay above the troughs, but ahead of the peaks." He checks his ground speed then the rear view mirror in his helmet. Already accelerating nicely. "Imagine your ass is a surfboard, make sure it's stuck into the face of the wave."

"A what?" Pet has no clue.

"A surfboard. They use them on Earth to ride big water waves. Ever seen a video of that?"

"Yes, sure. But I'm not sure I understand how they do it." There are no bodies of water on Mars much bigger than crater reservoirs and cisterns.

Marco has only seen videos of surfing back on Earth, but they have always been compelling for him. If he had grown up with all that water, he would have been a surfer not a pilot. "Look, think of a wave diagram. Stay in the middle. Don't slide down into the trough ahead of you, and don't let the peak behind you catch up. Got it?"

"Um, yeah. I think I can visualize that. What happens if I fall out?"

Marco is not paying close enough attention to his own flying while he explains how to fly. His variometer starts to beep as the wave face begins to lift him up. He smashes his speed bar as far forward as it will go and the beeping slows down. When a moment of equilibrium occurs, he checks his ground speed. His HUD displays an estimate of 122 kilometers per hour. This is just the start. The two of them will fly faster as they get more distance from the peak.

"If you hit the trough, you'll sink. There will be some turbulence, nothing you can't handle, but you're out of the race if that happens so just fly it to the ground and start running. Or lose some elevation and start looking for another thermal. If your variometer starts to scream, punch speed bar. Go as fast as you can until it levels out. Don't go over the back," Marco warns. "And, check your ground speed. The wave will gradually speed up most of the day. I'm showing 122 KPH."

Marco looks in his mirror again and sees Pet above and behind him. He turns to look over his shoulder to get a better idea of Pet's position on the wave. "Punch bar Pet! Punch it!" He commands.

Pet's glider lurches forward and speeds up as it descends rapidly. At least he responds quickly, Marco thinks. Marco could see that Pet's glider was meters away from the peak of the wave they are both riding. Had it crossed above that boundary layer, Pet would have been lucky if he could deploy his reserve. Marco knows the lines suspending the pilots below the gliders aren't made for that kind of stress. They can snap randomly, turning the aerodynamic shape of the wing into a flat-spin plummet-machine that is likely to get in the way of a reserve deployment.

"Stay away from the upper boundary layer. Sink out if you've got to, but stay away from the peak of the wave."

"Got it, got it. Mind if I fly beside you?"

"Not at all. Makes it easier, actually."

Pet's dive down the wave speeds him up and he slides into some air space just south of Marco. He tweaks his wing for a bit, trying to match speed with

Marco, eventually finding the sweet spot where he is able to carve back and forth across the face of the invisible mountain of moving air.

"Shit, Marco! Have you seen how fast we're going? Have you done this before?"

Marco smiles as wide as his helmet will allow. "Yes, I've tried this crossing four times already. On the second and third attempts, I nearly made it to the base of Olympus. I landed near the cliff barrier at the northern edge of the mountain. The last time, I was able to climb part way up the volcano."

"What about the first time?"

"I went right over the top of the first wave I caught. Tumbled into my lines and had to deploy the reserve. Tossed my laundry and got lucky, really lucky."

"Yeah I'll say. You went into your lines? How'd you deploy your reserve?" Marco cannot see Pet's face but his concern, and maybe some disbelief, is carried in his voice.

"This high up, I had some time to get out of the lines and glider. The worst part was after I deployed the reserve, I was able to recover the wing. It inflated and wanted to fly, and I had to pull in on the B-lines to get down. That trip was a real education. My suit wasn't up to being on the surface that long either."

Pet's curiosity has been perked, and he asks "Any one of those flights must have been a distance record, had to be. Why didn't you post your flights? I mean, no one else has even mentioned them."

"I never posted the track logs for fear of giving away the technique. The first flight was trash anyway, and I was trying to figure out the wave so that I could ride it in the GMT. The only other person who knows about those is my wife, Emma, and that's because she was on retrieve. If you can stay with me, you're going to get credit for flying the gap first. Even the Buckle." Marco grimaces a little when he says this, but then reflects Pet must have a pair. Attempting this race with nothing much to go on except the idea that Marco might show him the way. He decides Pet deserves credit as much as anyone and maybe a little respect.

"You're a legend in my book, Marco. I'm happy just flying with you. 'Burn the records', eh?" Pet quotes something Marco said after he broke the foot launched flight distance record the first time, turning the meaning upside down.

TRUCKS

Grace is sitting in the co-pilot seat holding a cat doll in one hand and a teacup in the other. She has an inventive and playful imagination, which she is using right now to facilitate a conversation between the cat and the cup.

"Catty is wanta cuppa tea?" Emma understands what Grace is trying to say. "No tank you. Catty no wanta eat my head please."

"Would Catty like a ting, do you think?" The driving has mellowed out a bit and Emma can split her attention between the road and her daughter.

"No, Mommy. Teacup no wanta ting. See?" Grace lifts the teacup and the cat doll and then cracks them together as if giving herself a toast. "Oh! He he he." Crack. "Oh!"

"Oh, you're such a comedian," Emma reaches over the center console of the rover and kisses her daughter on the head. This segment of the Daedalia plain is an arching dome of cryptogamic soils and engineered pinion and juniper trees intersected periodically with runoff arroyo. Emma knows from experience that she can take the rover as fast as it will travel along the dirt trail, only pausing to cross the occasional rock scarp or wash gully.

She imagines that Marco will be entering the mountain wave about now. Since the start of the race early this morning, she has been trying to cover the distance between the shield volcanoes so that when Marco lands later in the day, she will be close enough to aid him. She has already passed a number of support vehicles pulled off the side of the road, waiting near where they think their pilots might land after Ascraeus Mons.

The rover rocks on its struts as she clears the top of a round hill and begins to descend toward the next steep arroyo kilometers ahead. Emma engages the engine to brake the big vehicle. Occasionally, she must touch a foot the brake pedal to further slow the rover. Along this slope, the trees grow densely and tall, often blocking her view of the twisting dirt road ahead. The autopilot is useless here in these rolling hills.

Now Grace is flying the teacup from her perch within the bubble canopy of the rover. She makes whooshing motor sounds to accompany their passage over the red packed soil.

"Mama, you gonna radio Daddy? He gonna be fly'en."

"No, baby. Not this time." Marco had warned her not to risk radio contact until later in the day, only after he had flown the greater part of the gap between Ascraeus and Olympus Mons. Some of the support crews would have people listening during the whole race. Some would even broadcast false or misleading information along the route in an effort slow or divert their competition. Emma scowls at this, knowing it for a mode of behavior brought here from Earth. Cheating and bending the truth for a buck, she thinks to herself.

"Is Daddy up there?" Grace points up through the bubble canopy toward the pink and yellow sky above.

"Yes, baby. Daddy is up there. But you can't see him yet, can you?"

"I just wanta give him kisses."

"Me too, me too. Daddy will be back at the rover tonight." Let's hope. Emma dreads when Marco flies the mountain wave. She knows it is risky and, despite Marco's assurances, she knows there is very little he might do in the event of a major failure. She has tried and failed to talk him out of soaring the wave. "We'll give him kisses then. Okay?"

"Yes. One, two, tree kisses. Okay, Mama?"

Emma notices a collection of vehicle rooftops sticking through the dense junipers on the switchback below. She slows her rover as she approaches the last turn. Parked there, in the middle of the narrow road preventing her forward progress, are three support rovers. The tail truck has a big number "2" and Rebel Gliders logos all over its black and red hull. Emma cannot see the lead rig, its cabin is obscured by the other rovers parked between.

Emma reaches across the bubble cabin and over Grace, switching on the radio and picking up a headset from its cradle.

"Rebel Two, this is the UFMS rover De la Cosa. Do you read?"

The radio squelches twice, but no one responds.

"Once again Rebel Two, this is the UFMS rover De la Cosa. Please respond."

She waits, counting under her breath to twenty and this time, no one even bothered to squelch the microphone.

"Looks like we need to suit up, little girl." Emma says to big, round toddler eyes under curly black hair.

"Oh, Mommy, I wanta go outside."

"Yes, let's get you into your suit. After Mommy checks your seals, you can open the airlock if you'd like."

"Yes, I gonna do that cause I'm a big girl."

Emma backs up the rig and then pulls it off the dirt track. With the De la Cosa safely parked, she and Grace shuffle to the environmental suit locker just ahead of their bedroom. Emma opts to stuff Grace into her suit first, knowing the little girl would lose interest if she dresses herself first. Suiting up a toddler into an environmental suit is difficult enough all on its own. Putting one on a toddler who would rather be playing in the bubble cabin is impossible.

"Okay, Grace. Will you hold your helmet and gloves for me while I get my suit on?"

"Yes, Mama. I wanta hold them cause I'm big girl, huh?"

"You are a big girl." Emma slid into her utility suit quickly. She had been doing this since she was Grace's age, and it is second nature to her now. Snapping her boot cuffs closed, she asks, "Can you try and get your gloves on too?"

Grace sits down in the hallway and begins to pull her gloves over her hands, the left on the right hand and the right on the left. "Gloves don't fit. See?" she says, holding up her hands.

Emma tosses her gloves into the helmet and bends over her daughter. "Almost got them. Here, let Mama help."

Soon she is ushering the two of them into the airlock. Emma checks Grace's seals a second time and they ting helmets together before Emma lifts Grace up to cycle the airlock. Grace giggles into her microphone as the air pumps suck out the breathable atmosphere of the rover to replace it with a gush of Martian soup from outside.

Emma tethers Grace to her belt on a retractable line after the two of them hop down from the rover. They walk toward the rear of the line of stalled vehicles. The second rover in line belongs to Team Advanced, a version of the Rebel Gliders' red and black, but in blue, green, and white. The lead vehicle, which slid sideways into the arroyo at the bottom of this descent, sports a big Rebel One over black and red. A group of people stand on the steep bank of the drainage above the stricken rover.

Emma sets her suit radio to scan the band because there is not any chatter on the reserved suit-to-suit channel. Soon enough, she encounters a conversation and dials her radio in so she can talk with these people.

"Don't think it will be possible to get a rover around this mess," says a male voice. It is an incomplete statement, Emma waits for a response.

A woman's voice replies, "We'll see. Our third rover is rolling. That's good. Let's just wait these guys out. See what happens." A helmet turns toward Emma and Grace. "Looks like we have our first visitors." The suited figure makes a gesture toward the control surface mounted on her chest. She twists a dial until the screen reads "15 suit open".

Emma waves at the figure and adjusts her radio. Grace clutches her leg.

"Hello, can we help you?" Says the female voice on the open channel.

"I tried to raise someone in your caravan, but got no answer." Emma senses that there is something wrong with this situation. She decides to keep her plans to herself. "I'm trying to get through to Ulysses Fossae. Looks like someone got stuck?"

"Yes, we've got a rig that slid sideways into that gully." The woman walks up to her and Emma can now make out her face. It is Kerry Armstrong, Greg Neal's head coach.

"We've got recovery equipment on board my rover and a winch." Grace is hugging Emma's leg tight.

"Oh, I think we can handle it. We've got three rovers and one of them made it through before that one got stuck. They should be at Ulysses Fossae in an hour at most."

"Have you tried radioing the Fossae? I've got to get around here soon. I've even got a sat phone if the radio won't work." Emma tries.

Twelve figures in suits are spreading out behind and around Emma and Grace while she and Kerry talk.

"No, honey. I don't think so." Armstrong prowls into Emma's personal space. It is obvious that she has recognized Emma and these people playing some sort of game.

Quickly, Emma pushes Grace behind her for protection with her right hand and, raising her left, she keeps Armstrong at a distance.

"You see, I know who you are. That rig is wrecked there for a reason." Armstrong pushes her shoulder into Emma's hand.

"Back off, lady!"

Then a strange voice cuts in this conversation over the radio. "How about the suit channel? Hello, anyone listening down there?"

Another rover pulls into the space beside the De la Cosa. Witnesses. Emma wants to sneer at Armstrong, but holds onto her newly acquired distaste for this manipulative woman. She responds, "Hello, this is Emma Aguilar with Red Wings. Looks like there is a wreck ahead. Who is this?"

"Oh, hey! We've been trying to catch you on the radio all day. This is Ivan with Pavonis Universal. Our boy, Pet, has been tagging along with Marco."

"Who?"

"Petrus Mandel, another racer. From the University. He left the airlock with Marco and has been with him since. We can't get either one of them to acknowledge us on the radio."

Emma bends down and picks up Grace. Holding the little girl on her hip, she glares at the two Earth-men blocking her way back toward the De la Cosa. They part after a moment and let her through.

"I'm coming aboard, Ivan, if that's okay with you?" Emma growls.

"Yeah, sure. It's crowded, but come on in." Two figures, in the Pavonis cab, wave at Emma and Grace through the glass as they near.

Climbing aboard with Grace, she cycles the airlock. Grace buries her face mask into Emma's chest. "I so scared, Mama. Why they pushin' you?"

The inner hatch opens and Emma sets Grace down, shuts the portal behind her, and then pulls off Grace's helmet. Her helmet comes off next, and then she picks up Grace and tries to console her. "I'm sorry, baby. I'm so sorry, we're safe now. It's going to be okay, it's going to be okay." It is difficult to swallow her rage and fear, but she holds her daughter and looks at the occupants of the Pavonis rover. Two college-aged boys crowd into a tiny living space split between the driving cabin, a messy kitchenette, and a pile of gear mounded on a tiny couch.

The one in the co-pilot's couch says, "There's a bigger problem than a wrecked rover, isn't there?"

Emma recognizes his voice from the radio, it is Ivan. "Yes. That's Team Rebel, and they're trying to keep us from reaching Marco this evening. I think they wrecked that rover on purpose."

"They what?"

"They wrecked that rover to keep me from reaching Marco. And if your guy is flying with Marco, him too."

"Why is the little girl so upset?"

"Armstrong threatened us when we left our rover. Bunch of Earth goons. I can't believe this."

Ivan sits down in the co-pilot's chair, then turns his chair toward the navigation console to his right. "Hold on, I've got an idea. How stuck is their rig?"

"Pretty stuck, and it doesn't look like they are going to do anything to move it any time soon. Armstrong said they had another rover out in front of the wreck."

Ivan sorts through satellite imagery and charts of Daedalia. His hands gesture in front of the screen, moving objects and images around. He waves his fingers and then starts to draw over the imagery.

"This is where we are. Look here, if we backtrack a little and loop around to the north, there is a mining road that comes around the head of this arroyo. It might be slower going, but it should only set you back," he pauses to make the calculation in his head, "maybe 40 minutes at most."

"Ivan, that works but that mining road comes out just on the other side of the wreck." Emma points at the location from over his shoulder. "How are we going to keep them from interfering when we turn back?"

Ivan rubs his chin, then the other kid speaks up from the pilot's seat. "Um, Misses Aguilar. I'm Devon. I think I can take care of that."

CRUSH

Emma and Grace go back to the De la Cosa. She makes them a small lunch of cheese and crackers with some grapes. Grace loves grapes enough that she seems to have forgotten Emma's run-in with Armstrong. Emma darkens the bubble canopy all the same, no need to remind her daughter of the danger just outside their door.

They have decided to wait a bit before they make any move to let Armstrong and her crew settle down. But once the lunch ends, Emma puts Grace in her safety seat and straps her in snugly then she radios over to the Pavonis rover on a private channel.

"Pavonis, this is De la Cosa. We're ready to backtrack. See you in a bit." She does not wait for their reply. Instead she starts the drive engine, revving it hard, then clears the bubble canopy instantly turning the dome transparent. The crews from the two parked rovers and a third wrecked one scramble towards airlocks.

Emma looks to her left, into the bubble canopy of the Pavonis rover, where Devon and Ivan jump around making wild faces. Evidently, they have amended their plans a bit, screaming and hollering at the suited figures racing to get into their rovers.

Once everyone has stepped into an airlock, Devon raises a thumb and grins maniacally back across the narrow space between. "You have a mean streak, Devon," she says as she slams the De la Cosa into reverse.

Devon hoots into the radio and then hammers the accelerator hard, driving his rover straight at the rear of the parked Rebel vehicle. The sound of the crashing rovers is audible through the pressure glass. Unfortunately, Emma is not able to see Devon run the University rover's forward push plate into the red rig, but the noise is cathartic as he enthusiastically urges the line of vehicles toward the wreck and the arroyo. Unable to take any action in response, their crews are stuck inside airlocks until the pumps complete their cycle.

Then over the open suit channel, Devon heckles, "You don't mess with Martian Mamas, mud suckers. Go back to Earth if you want to play that way."

Emma turns the De la Cosa around at the first switchback and then makes a rush for the mining road.

MARS JETS

"What an amazing race this year has turned out to be. I'm Bill Vance and, with me, is Toma Crysta bringing you the latest on the 2111 Grand Martian Tour." The camera captures two suited men sitting at their shiny desk, behind them is a montage of images from the course.

"That is correct, Bill, we're seeing history in making. A pair of little-known Martians has taken significant lead, breaking with tradition, and making course judges work overtime. MBS has had to scramble to keep up with Marco Aguilar and Pet Mandel because they are currently soaring higher and faster than hovercam can. There is jet circling above them only to keep camera on these racers."

The camera changes to an image of two arcing parafoils flying in the distance; they are highlighted by long rays of the setting sun and a backdrop of dark, thin atmosphere near space.

"We've got word that these two competitors have, today, set a distance record for paragliding on Mars. Throughout the solar system. And they're still going as the sun begins to set on this first day of the GMT. MBS has some amazing footage captured of this race as we've been following these amazing Martians from a high altitude jet," says the voice of Bill Vance. "Early this morning, teams were forced into making a gamble, launch early and follow or stick to tradition and lose. A truly inspirational flight in a weather phenomenon no one knew man could survive."

"And Bill," cuts in Crysta, "Gamble paid off for only a few. Franz Wickenhauser played it safe and ran on course all the way to Gaisburg. He is already on ground and running again, but has little chance of finishing on the podium. Then there were other racers, like Greg Neal, who saw what was happening and tried to launch from tundra on eastern slope of Ascraeus Mons."

The camera switches from the image of two pilots gliding in the setting sun to an animation of the race. A line of runner icons sprouts into wings along the side of the volcano. Lines behind the icons of the fliers show some ascending in weak thermal uplifts along the face of the mountain, but most of them sinking out down the side of the great hill.

Crysta continues, "The first test of day was finding lift. Neal has three second place finishes in GMT, and you can see he is working overtime to catch up with upstarts." A paraglider icon and its following line are highlighted as it spirals madly to clear the cone. It and several others climb into the mountain wave.

"The second test of day is mountain wave. Bill, back in my day, no one thought you could soar slow aircraft, like paraglider, in weather like mountain wave. You can see that of all racers who flew to wave, only few figured out how to make it work." Neal's highlighted line and three others continue on west while nine or ten glider icons plummet from about the same spot in the sky.

"That's right, Toma." The camera changes to a hovercam image of a jumbled wing and a man falling like a rock. Five seconds into the video, an arm reaches out of the collapsed wing and throws a white package attached to a long coil of lines. The reserve parachute quickly inflates turning into a dome above the man arresting his fall. "Of the fourteen pilots that made it into the mountain wave, only four were able to fly in it. And of the ten who then fell out three of them deployed their reserve chutes. That mountain wave is risky business, Toma."

The camera is back on the animation that has caught up to the present. Aguilar and Mandel are out in front with Neal following lower and kilometers behind in third. Scattered loosely across the plains west of Ascraeus Mons, and well behind the leaders still in the air, are the remnants of the race. Most of which have made dirt and are now running across the plains.

The camera focuses back on the two men at the lead. Toma Crysta explains, "Some racers, who went to dirt early, have given up. There are a number that are going to try to complete race, but even more who have checked back in at Tharsis."

CRATER CHECK IN

"You there, Emma?" Marco is on the sat-phone with his wife and support crew of one.

"Yeah, baby. You're coming in loud and clear." She replies into his ear.

"Not sure if you can see us yet, but the sun is going down fast and I've got the blinky on."

"Good. You both made it?"

It takes Marco a moment to catch up with her. "This student followed me out the airlock and down to the scarp? He's been keeping up all day long."

"Are you annoyed?" She asks knowingly.

"Yeah, at first, I was. He's grown on me a little. Nice kid. Just a FYI," Marco pauses to look beneath at the landing site he's shooting for, "I don't think his support crew kept up today. When we broke radio silence he couldn't reach them. We'll have a guest for dinner."

"I'm way ahead of you, baby. Listen, keep it quiet when you come through the airlock. Grace is down for the night and I don't want you to wake her up."

"No problem, honey. I'll let Pet know. What's for dinner?"

"Fresh salad with some aquaculture tuna, plenty of water, and O2. Can you drop a pin near where you're going to land? I still can't see you and the trees are growing pretty thick down here."

Marco draws a finger across his flight deck, an icon lights up on his HUD visor. He moves it around until it is over the site, a medium sized clearing in some Krumholtz-GMO pines. When he lifts his finger, there is a flag sticking out of the ground, painted over the location in his HUD. He pushes a couple of buttons and then fires it off to Emma.

"Let me know when you get that. I'm not sure if there is a vehicle route up there. Can you plot one?" He says into the microphone.

"Umm, huh, no." She pauses a moment. Thinking out loud, she asks, "Can you guys land and make your way here?" Another flag appears in his HUD.

Marco responds, "Yep, shouldn't be a problem. Maybe an hour, give or take. We'll be running through the night once we resupply. Erm, or at least I intend to, not sure about Pet."

"Alright, love. Lights will be on when you get here. Keep it quiet, please. She's out cold. Lots of excitement today." She pauses a moment, then says, "Oh wait, I can see your blinky. Talk to you soon, bye now." She blows kisses for effect and cuts the line.

The sun has sunk below the horizon when Marco and Pet have finished packing up their wings and set out in the direction of Marco's support vehicle. The two of them jog along the Martian surface, weaving in and out of stands of low trees and compact brush in the dark for about 40 minutes.

Pet is breathing hard again and not talking much as, together, they cross the undulating country at the foot of Olympus Mons.

Marco checks their speed in his HUD and wonders to himself if Pet will be able to keep up during the night run? His breathing has been labored at times and his pace periodically slows.

Marco attempts to stoke his enthusiasm. "Wow! 1,200 km." A couple of breaths. "Did you see the jet they sent up to video us?" He knows that his intensity seems contrived and maybe a little forced.

Pet responds immediately, despite what sounds like labored breathing. "Oh yes, I saw them." Pause for a breath. "Wahoo!" Pet jumps a little and kicks his heels together at the distance record. "Checked the MBS broadcast a couple of times too." Another deep breath. "Neal is on our tail." Breath. "That guy is a monster, we're going to have to move."

Silence again falls between them as they reach the edge of a minor impact crater. Near the bottom is a small tarn and a white utility rover with its perimeter lights on. Marco points at the vehicle, turns to Pet with a smile and a gesture to come along. They bound down the slope of the crater together, a kind of skip which Martians use that is faster and safer than running.

Once there, Marco punches in the key code and they enter the airlock together. It cycles quickly and the two of them help each other to remove their helmets. Marco opens the inside of the lock as quietly as he can, and tiptoes around the door toward the kitchen where Emma is standing. She turns to them both and puts a finger to her lips.

With all three of them in the tiny kitchen, Emma closes the hallway door leading to the rear of the vehicle. She whispers, "So good to meet you, Pet." Gestures to the table where two big bowls of greens wait.

Both Marco and Pet dig into the meal with gusto. Emma slides into the little booth and kisses Marco on the cheek as he gobbles up the food. She relaxes her noise discipline a tad when she asks, "So what are you guys short on for tonight?"

"My suit has been recycling pretty well all day, but I might want to top off the aux-tank before we go. Also, going to need a refill on the goo and water." Marco takes a look at some readouts on his wrist. "Yep. Water for sure, honey. And I know I packed the raspberry flavored goo, but do we have any chocolate in the cabinet?"

Emma looks at Pet, who looks surprised. She recites the adage, "On Mars we'll do it together," in order to dispel any of Pet's reluctance. "What do you need, Pet?"

Pet swallows a mouthful of salad then says, "Oh yes, um, suit says some O2 for main and aux."

Marco looks across the tiny table at his new race companion. "Sure that's all you need?" He raises an eyebrow. "We've got to cover about 50 km tonight and be ready to launch tomorrow morning. Neal can do that and then some without blinking. There's no resupply after we exit this crater."

"Um, okay," responds Pet, "Then I could use some food and water too. Maybe a battery change, if you've got a spare." He pauses thinking, searching for the right words. "You mean you're not going to ditch me on the run?"

"I already tried that. Doubt I could if I wanted to. So don't come up with excuses that will slow us down later, right?"

Pet's smile spreads across his face like it was spilled. "Okay, then. Okay."

They finish their dinner and repack their suits with the necessary items. Marco and Pet take turns checking each other's supplies and suit functions.

RESUPPLY

"Greg Neal is being resupplied," booms the voice of Bill Vance, "before he begins gobbling up the distance separating him from what he hopes is his first victory in the Grand Martian Traverse."

The camera recounts an episode of resupply madness; the hands and arms of his support team in the confines of a plush rover cover Neal. He's yelling commands at people down a hallway out of sight from the cameras.

"Get that water ready, Mel. It should have been ready to go when I got to the airlock. Jesus!" Neal is annoyed and anxious to get going.

His face is etched with anger and determination. A woman turns his chin in her direction so she can gain his full attention. Someone else stands in front of the camera lens momentarily blocking the view.

The broadcast switches back to Vance and Crysta. "That is Team Rebel head coach, Kerry Armstrong," says Toma Crysta. "They must discuss overland strategy and potential resupply along way. Neal does not want to give up any advantage."

"The pressure is on for Team Rebel. Isn't it, Toma?"

"You better believe it, Bill," replies Toma Crysta. The camera switches to a dark field with a slightly lighter starry sky above and two headlamps bobbing along in the distance under the stars. "Neal spent most of day playing follow-the-leader with Marco Aguilar and Petrus Mandel who have been attached at hip since they left airlock at Tharsis. In last hour and half of flight, Neal was able to make up some much needed time and now stands poised to catch these two upstarts before sunrise tomorrow."

The camera cycles again to an image of Greg Neal leaving the air lock, head-lamp blazing and trekking poles propelling him forward. "And this is Neal's strongest hand. Before he got started doing endurance soaring style racing, he was a well-regarded ultra distance runner. Isn't that correct, Toma?"

"This is correct, Bill. Neal has taken home first place finishes in many of Earth's more challenging foot races. With the reduced gravity on Mars, he has advantage in muscle mass and conditioning that Aguilar and Mandel cannot match."

The camera lifts up and pans out, catching the light of Neal's headlamp illuminating the dust he's kicking up as he flies toward his quarry.

FATIGUE

"Listen, Marco. At his current rate, he'll catch us by day break. Just go, I must be slowing you down." Pet's voice contains a modicum of panic in it.

"No, you listen. You can't break out that old Martian dictum and expect me to not hear you. Korima! Pet, you know how it works. I'm running about as fast as I can right now anyway. So you either keep up or drop out. But it's your decision. Keep up."

There is silence, or what will pass for it, on the radio while Pet mulls this over. His breathing has been ragged at times, especially when they climb. And as the night wears on, there will be more and more climbing ahead of them. Pet is exhausted too. He's been trying to distract himself from the pain he's feeling — the result of the run and his desire to sleep — by catching up on MBS broadcasts of the race overlaid in his helmet's HUD.

Perhaps that was a poor choice. He reaches across his body, with his right hand, and toggles off the bad news. Neal is catching them. Why won't Marco just go? Pet is worried that his slowness will become the reason for a loss at the finish line.

Marco cuts into his thoughts over the radio. "You're thinking about how much it hurts, right? Deep down, under all that doubt, it hurts. We're Martians and we're not made for this. Neal is a hulking beast compared to the two of us.

He's got muscles on his muscles and a bone density we can only dream of. Guess what, Pet, that's the way the Neanderthals went. Too much muscle, too much bone. Neal has been stopping for resupply all night. We've been running and he's been resupplied."

Marco has slowed a little to deliver this message. "It will do you no good to wish you were Neal, any more than it's going to do you any good to wish you were me. You kept up with me all day yesterday. You flew a mountain wave and made a new distance record. You did that."

Marco sounds a little angry now. "You can choose to succumb to those feelings of self doubt and the pain. Or you can put a cap on them and reach for some glory. It's in reach. Less than 15 kilometers until we get to where I want to launch. Just fucking reach."

Marco sends a flag icon to Pet's wrist computer, it lights up in his HUD high above them.

They continue to shuffle through the red and tan soils of the gradually altered Mars. Pet's breathing has steadied on the radio. The first hint of pre-dawn light illuminates the hulking mass of Olympus Mons before them. They can neither see the sides of the massive volcano, hidden beyond the low horizon, or its summit.

In silence, Pet reaches behind himself and detaches a pair of trekking poles from the bottom of his pack. While inserting his hands through the wrist loops, he takes a couple of deep pulls from the drinking tube in his helmet.

He plants his poles and kicks his feet, painting a grin across his lips in the hope that it will return some motivation to his body. He catches up with Marco and the two of them begin to mount the next series of hills side by side.

They zig-zag up talus slopes covered in scree and volcanic ejecta. Periodically, they change places with Pet taking the lead for a while. And then, just when he thinks he cannot go any longer, Marco takes over and his cadence seems to pull Pet along for a while.

The flag is growing in size as they near a false summit of the volcano's lower cliff skirting. Pet looks back down the alluvial fan they've just ascended as they jog along the edge of the cliff towards a pair of vehicles parked a couple hundred meters above. His support team must have been in contact with Emma last night because there is a big Pavonis Universal logo on the flank of one of those rovers. Glancing down the alluvial fan again, he's not sure, but he thinks he can make out a tiny light climbing up the slope below.

DUST IN WIND

"Near the quickest finish ever the race is heating up. Greg Neal is less than a kilometer behind the leaders, Mandel and Aguilar. That Rebel is a Devil and he wants this race back." Bill Vance appears self-satisfied with his play on words. He turns to Toma Crysta on his left.

Crysta raises his eyebrow at Bill Vance, but still takes his turn in their banter. "Bill, Greg Neal has put on amazing display of speed during night. Mandel and Aguilar made it to their resupply vehicles about fifteen minutes ago, and Neal is climbing a cut in cliff apron surrounding Olympus Mons."

The camera breaks away to a view of a racer in red and black climbing up rocks. He's just beneath the rim of a very large cliff. There are two vehicles parked above the edge and a third is making its way up to that shared spot. "That's Neal's headlamp just below the edge. I'm told that Mandel and Aguilar have just come out the airlock of their own support vehicles. Without the aid of the sun last night, all these racers will need to restock on air. They'll probably take on water and food as well. Once the sun comes up, their bio-reactor suits will pick up production again," says Vance, explaining the scene on camera.

Two figures separate from a line of vehicles, they walk over near the edge of the cliff and begin to unpack their paragliders. They're moving independently from one another, going through their own routine, making ready for a launch and the flight up the side of Olympus Mons.

"And, Bill, today's race is all about climbing," pronounces Toma Crysta, again in the focus of the camera. "Olympus Mons is largest mountain in solar system."

"I'm wondering if Mandel and Aguilar have any other wild cards to pull from their sleeves today, Toma. Yesterday's record breaking flight from the side of Ascraeus was impressive and certainly upset the plans of many racers, but will it be enough to get them over the finish line ahead of the passion and drive Greg Neal demonstrated last night?"

Two figures stand motionless with their backs facing east towards the rising sun now. At the left hand side in the field of view, another figure comes into frame. This one unpacks his wing while his support team stuffs supplies into his suit. He throws a pair of trekking poles away, discarding them as dead weight. Other objects are presented to him and then tossed to the side. He looks rushed compared to the two stoic figures standing motionless nearby.

One of the still figures bends over and picks something up from near his feet.

The newcomer is trying to fly his wing already as the first riffles of rising air begin to creep up the side of the great mountain. Immediately, his wing comes up over his head and he turns and runs off the edge of the cliff. His wing sinks and he moves back and forth across the face of the cliff trying to stay airborne. Scratching for any lift in the light air.

The other two figures have not moved from their roost, waiting patiently for the right moment. Their moment. When a bubble of rising air will present itself and take them up and up. Periodically, one of them reaches down and lifts up a handful of fine soil. Letting it slide between his fingers, it falls straight down, once, then again, and yet again.

Now two-hundred meters below is the pilot who rushed to launch. Still descending. As if in slow motion, he slides gently down the cliff face.

Now Marco's fully illuminated figure bends down once more. He lifts the dirt and lets it fall. It falls at an angle indicating the incoming breeze, the lifting air. Marco turns to Pet, nods once, and lifts his lines. His wing rises quickly overhead with a snap and a ruffle as the high tech fabric inflates and the aerodynamic shape comes to life.

Marco pauses with his hands on his break toggles, seeming almost to play with the wing and the wind, as the camera looks on. He dances beneath the canopy shifting back and forth to stay centered under the flying body.

Pet's wing comes up in a cloud of dust and his feet are dragged under the arcing parafoil. He struggles to slow the forward progress of the wing above by extending the break lines as far down as they will go. It is lift, a thermal grabs him and shoots him into the air. He twists around momentarily helpless under his flying wing, but then sits back in the harness and soars.

Below them, Neal has found lift too. He cannot turn into it yet, being too close to the cliff face, but takes advantage of it just the same flying back and forth in the rising air and climbing slowly back toward the summit far above.

Pet is climbing fast, at least five hundred meters above the edge of the cliff now. Marco is still playing with his wing on the cliff, kiting it above him a little left and then a little right. Someone new runs out from the most recent rover arrival with a camera, pointing it up at the orange and green canopy being danced across the talus.

Hovercams and scouting drones are converging on the site, some of them break off from the scene at the cliff's edge to follow Pet ever higher into the atmosphere. A few are even below Neal's wing trying to get a shot of all three pilots at once. But the majority swarm around the stationary aesthetic of the glider being danced at the edge of the vast cliff.

And then, with all eyes focused on his joy in the rising sun, Marco stops playing. He turns, bends deeply at the waist and takes two big steps towards the edge turning into a bird man, elegant and swift, suspended under his wing.

Immediately, he's found lifting air, his gyre is tight and centered over the invisible column. A pendulum beneath his turning canopy, his body rotates outside the center of the spiraling glider. The energy in this thermal is visible, Marco's rise up and away from the cliff side is quick and accelerating. Soon he is circling in tandem with Pet. Below, Neal is climbing slowly.

Dynamic Lines

An incoming call is beeping in Pet's ear, it is Greg Neal's name flashing in his HUD. "Marco, Neal is calling me. Should I talk to him?" He asks over their radio channel.

"Hell yes! Dude can't fly, but he can run. See if you can psych him out a bit."

Pet switches on the call, "Yeah?"

There is a low rumble of a chuckle then, "I've got you both beat. Make sure you tell that to your friend. Your support boys have made sure of that." Neal laughs menacingly into the microphone.

Pet stammers out a response. "We'll see about that mud sucker. Um, go back to Earth." He closes the line with Neal and reopens the channel with Marco.

"That didn't go so well," he says to Marco. "He was calling to psych me out. I never know what to say."

"Yeah, yeah. Of course, you've seen the games these guys play." Marco can look across the thermal they are both turning in and see Pet's face. "We've got this, Pet. We've got this."

Marco looks down to see that Neal is in a separate column of rising air, his vertical rise is not as fast as theirs and he's falling increasingly behind.

"Look, he's falling behind." But then Pet notices one of several camera drones orbiting them in his peripheral vision. The drone tilts steeply and begins to move rapidly toward Pet. "Watch out!"

Pet sees the drone heading for his lines and leans into a hard high-banked turn. The drone's six-hover propellers slice through the empty air where Pet was just soaring, narrowly missing the thin lines that suspend him under the wing.

The small hovering craft is buffeted as it penetrates the boundary of the thermal column of air the two pilots turn in. It pauses to find a point of equilibrium before tilting once more, quickly beating the air toward Marco's lines this time.

Moving fast, the machine cannot alter its course quickly enough to collide with their lines, but it passes much too close for comfort. Marco loses the lift, and his variometer drones in his ear indicating the sinking air he has passed into to avoid the big hover camera.

Someone has seen the erratic behavior of the camera drone because the power to the semi-autonomous vehicle is abruptly cut. It drops like a stone past Marco as he searches for the thermal in the open volume of thinning air.

AGENCY

"Toma, we received word from race officials confirming the rogue camera drone which we just saw pitching into race leaders, Aguilar and Mandel, has been deactivated. XtremeVideo, an independent Earth-based media group, owns the camera. Their spokesperson is fielding questions but, so far, no one knows what caused the malfunction. And no one knows what might happen, the rules don't cover this."

"This is true, Bill. This type of intrusion is unprecedented. Aguilar and Mandel still climbing, but can they stay ahead of Neal? No one knows," says Crysta indifferently.

An image of the two race leaders flickers across the field of view as they turn above the massive volcano Olympus Mons.

"Let's look at that again, can we? Just one more time," intones Bill Vance. The image is switched to a replay of the rogue drone diving toward Mandel as it passes by the lines of his left wing. "You see how close that comes to Mandel's lines? You know, Toma, had it only happened once, I think we could assume it was an accident. Something wrong with the drone, but watch," Vance pauses in his explanation as the drone stabilizes in the air, "it stops, then takes aim and makes another pass. That was deliberate, had to be."

Crysta's tone borders on uncivil, and it is apparent that he desires an end to this conversation. "Is premature to speculate, Mr. Vance. There is no doubt of unfortunate nature of encounter between pilots and drone."

The image on screen changes back to the two announcers at their polished desk. A mask of disbelief glares at Toma Crysta. Bill Vance continues, "Really, Toma? I'm sure that race officials will get to the bottom of this, but I know my eyesight has not gone. How might you explain the second pass then?"

"Camera drone is semi-autonomous vehicle with much complexity. Many problems may occur in complex system, yes?"

LAST GLIDE

Pet looks down then back in Marco's direction. "How we going to stay ahead of him at Buena Suerte?"

"First, we're going on glide to the airlock. All the way, buddy, so don't stop climbing once you reach the edge of the cone. You'll need some altitude to make it in there, but you're always going to glide faster than he can run."

"Okay, that's a start. Still have to make it into the city and across the line?" There is doubt in Pet's voice, but less than before.

"Yes, and there are too many locks for us to try and pinch him in the cycle. So hope he goes on glide early and needs to run some. Pack your wing quickly, and run like you've got everything to lose."

The hover cameras are starting to swarm again. Marco is annoyed as one comes very close to the outside set of lines suspending him under his wing. "Oh and remember, 'Burn the records'."

"Right!" says Pet, "Burn em."

BUENA SUERTE

Two lines of temporary fence create a funnel toward the eastern city airlocks of Buena Suerte. As the funnel narrows, inflatable arches, lighting towers, and communication booms have been erected crossing and blocking the way. In the past, racers have almost always landed at the edge of Olympus Mons' tremendous cone. They only have a temporary flight box down below the rim. There are almost always orbital flights taking off from and arriving at the space plane port on the far side of the crater and the port suspends operations while the fragile paragliders enter the cone. Marco searches for a place to land as close as he can get to the door.

There, between two inflatable arches, he thinks he can manage it. He calls to Pet, "I'm going to crab my way into that space between the Mercedes arch and the yellow one behind it. Where are you going?"

"Man, it's too tight. I can't stick it between those. I'm going to get hung up," responds Pet.

"Put it where you can, as close as you can."

"Okay. Going for that first row of towers, I can run it out under them if I need to."

"Gotcha," says Marco. He's a little above and behind Pet. Neal played it safe and landed out just below the crater rim. He was packing up his wing when they last saw him, preparing to run.

Pet aims straight down the funnel with, maybe, a little tailwind pushing him forward. It is an awkward landing, but Marco can see he is down and already scrambling to pack his wing up and move out.

Marco crabs back and forth, slipping sideways across the moving air, losing altitude as fast as he can. He turns tight, putting his glider into a spiral descent, coring the open space between the two pylons. Then braking hard centimeters above the pavement, his glider pops up overhead and momentarily stalls. He's left standing, with his wing deflating rapidly.

Quickly, Marco moves to detach the wing from his harness. He pulls the lines straight and together, then with his harness still strapped to him, he runs to a wing tip. Grabbing it by the leading edge, he runs in front of his glider, twirling it into a tube. The lines are slung into the cone of fabric and he folds the whole thing in on itself.

There is Pet, packed and standing before him. "Go!" Marco yells into the radio. "Run!" Pet moves without saying anything, momentarily hesitating, but then breaking into a sprint for the door.

Marco has his harness off, and is violently shoving the wing into this. Still shoving he starts to shuffle towards the lock, and through his helmet, he can make out the sound of the cheering rise from the crowd. They see Neal. Marco turns and looks up the funnel of a raceway, he sees Neal too.

The man bounds with each stride. The gravity of Mars is no impediment to him. His rig is packed tight and well, and the red and black of his suit blends with the Martian cliff behind him.

RUN! Marco screams at himself. Pet has the airlock door open, he turns to see Marco sprinting and slides an arm in front of the hatch sensor holding it open. Once through, Pet begins to cycle the lock. The two of them can hear the air pumping into the chamber as Marco finishes shoving his wing into his rucksack.

The inside door automatically unlocks and both men work either side of the exit, unlatching the door quickly and skillfully. It opens and they rush through the gate.

"He's calling again!"

"Shit, ignore him," Marco belches out. There's not enough air, his lungs are already burning.

Neal is through the gate and pushing his body hard, his great legs thump as they propel him over the ground. The crowd on either side of the road has erupted, cheering the racers on to the finish.

Marco can see Neal growing larger in his helmet mirror. He stops paying attention to the man behind only in time to see Pet right in front of him. The two of them collide, Marco placing a forward stride right into the back of one of Pet's legs. They topple, rolling together, meters before the finish line.

SECOND

"Amazing, amazing," booms the voice of Bill Vance. "This is race history, folks. Moments before crossing the line, Aguilar and Mandel have collided." The camera is focused on Aguilar in the green and orange. Mandel has fallen and rolled to the side. The green and orange suit is up and starts to make his way to the finish line. Then stops, turns, and jogs back to the prone Mandel, extending a hand.

"And there is Neal passing them. I can't believe what I'm seeing today." Bill Vance is in a frenzy of sportscaster announcement. "Never before, I've never seen anything like this. Aguilar just gave Neal the Big Red Buckle!" A red figure blurs in front of the camera momentarily, but the shot stays focused on the two races halted just before the finish line.

Mandel's white gloved hand reaches up and grasps the green clad hand of Aguilar. Aguilar pulls as a million flashes of light blossom along the street. Mandel is clearly injured, he limps, but Aguilar slides an arm around his waist and pulls Mandel's arm over his shoulder. The two of them walk the last few steps across the finish line together. The camera watches.

Bill Vance sums up the race, "On Mars, we do it together."

A Note from the Grinder

Thanks for reading my primer science fiction novelette. I sincerely hope you enjoyed The Big Red Buckle, which is the first in a series. Book number two, set within the "sports in space" theme, is due out spring of 2014. If you enjoyed this story about Marco and Pet you may be looking forward to my next novella "Up Slope".

Also, I would like to encourage you to send me your impressions. You're holding a chunk of the foundation of my writing career and your reviews, good or bad, will help me improve, grow as a writer, and reach new readers.

As a way to thank you for buying this book and for passing along your reviews — on Amazon, Goodreads, or through the social media outlet of your choosing — I have included an additional short story in the print version of "The Big Red Buckle." Currently, this series of shorts is also available on Amazon.

Check back often, I hope you're surprised and entertained, and that these stories transport you to another time and place for a little while.

JOULUPUKKI

On the first day of my seventh winter, my Father Oaván came into the tiny alcove that served as my room in the longhouse at the foot of the Frederikshaab glacier. My mother Florá stood looking concerned just beyond the threshold of the tiny room while Oaván spoke to me in his deep, reserved baritone.

"Birki, your mother and I have decided that today you will come and hunt the Joulupukki with the men."

Excitement raced through my blood, but I arrested this moment of childish glee knowing that it would betray me even as I was passing over the threshold into manhood.

"Thank you, Father. I will carry my spear alongside Thor. The winter buck will bleed for old Woden," I said with a cracking voice and leapt from the bedsheets.

Father Oaván mussed my hair and chuckled. "Carry your spear beside the longbeards, and take care not let it lay in the sand, and I am certain old Thor will see you through the hunt." He put a hand on my shoulder and turned me toward the shower down the hall. "But first, go clean yourself. Your stench will spook the buck."

I showered and dressed, then checked the reserve level on my facemask. I chose the tiny rucksack from the back of my wardrobe and took my felted wool hat and mittens, embroidered with my family's pattern of blueberries and vines and stuffed them into the big, front pocket of the long fur fringed anorak my mother had made for me. I slipped the scabbard from the narrow spade-head of my spear to inspect the edge I had been sharpening for a full Martian month. It gleamed in the light cast from the desk lamp on the far wall, and I smiled with satisfaction.

In the long hall I stacked my spear and ruck on the wall alongside the other weapons the men had brought before the hunt. Then I took my place next to Elnar and Guhtur at the far end of the table. My Father stood at its head wearing the red fur pants and horned helm.

"Onko täällä kilttejä lapsia? I doubt it. Good children live all along the equator. Ha!" Gathered around the table the men cheered at his wit. "Today we will hunt the Yule Buck. His blood will spill on our hearth fire and Woden will grant us another long Martian year of prosperity and happiness. Now eat your fill, for the hunt will be long and we cannot return until we have our goat."

Everyone cheered once more and dug into trenchers of food set before us on the polished stone. I heaped my plate with warm gahkko and smothered the flat cakes in lingon-berry sauce. I pocketed smoked fish in my anorak while shoveling the pancakes into my mouth. Father was right. Today would be a long, hard run and I did not want to fall behind the hunting pack.

Elnar noticed me slipping the fish into my pocket. "Hey, you're not supposed to do that," he hissed loud enough to turn some heads.

"Shut your mouth, Elnar! This is your first Joulupukki too. Watch the others." I directed his attention down the stone table using a fork loaded with pancake. "You're going to need the energy too."

"But my father says ..." he continued to whine before I cut him off.

"Watch!" I said through a mouth full of gahkko. "They all do it too." I pointed again at the longbeards down the table with my empty fork. "I know your father says that it isn't 'traditional.' But he's wrong, it's just not normal to talk about it."

Elnar slouched on the bench beside me. Guhtur added, "And it's never a good idea to rat out your friends. Come on, eat up and stuff your pockets."

I often felt sorry for Elnar. His parents had immigrated to the Southern Laplander Hinterlands and he was always awkward even when he tried to fit in. His father read the Eddas, but just like his factory-cut anorak Elnar always seemed made up, or put on. Elnar was stuck somewhere between my culture and his father's attempts to reclaim some part of his lost heritage.

The three of us watched as my Father Oaván reached a long arm across the head of the table to grab a handful of smoked reindeer meat, nibbling at briefly, before he tucked it into his pocket.

"That pocket smells more like salmon than anything else, but I see the reindeer is closer," I chuckled to my friends.

Breakfast completed, all the men tromped toward the air lock with hunting spears in hand. Elnar, Guhtur and I followed closely as groups of five or six stepped into the lock, donned their filter masks, and then set out into the dark polar winter. Solstice or not, the day would be short and cold.

The lock discharged us into a herd of longbeards. The hunters began separating into groups. My Father Oaván picked us out of the crowd saying, "You boys will run with me today." The he pointed north, towards the chaos, and said in a low whisper. "Let's go."

Father Oaván began trotting lightly over the barren tundra plain that met the edge of the cliff dwelling. His reindeer skin boots padded along quietly through the red dust just ahead of me and I felt my body begin to relax into the run. Elnar panted along behind me, and I did not need to see Guhtur periodically prodding him with the butt of his spear to know that my other friend followed close behind.

Near the edge of a slot canyon Father Oaván slowed and held up a hand. He crouched and began to crawl with his spear resting in the crook of his elbows. We followed his example, trying to calm the breath in our throats, knowing that he had seen something.

Father Oaván whispered to us. "Do you see it? A peikko lumbering down below."

I could make out the russet fur of the troll's thick mane only because of the white undercoat, which contrasted, with the red wall of the canyon below. It must have been stalking the canyons for goats too. It raised its head, scenting the air that ran through the bottom of the canyon. Guhtur raised his spear and began to pull the sheath from the head.

"Guhtur, that's a goat spear! Put it down, fool." snapped my Father.

We scrambled back away from the edge of the cliff and crouched beneath crooked pines. "That would have only angered the troll," he said to Guthur. "Birki, mark this location on your pad. Let's move on."

Everyone plucked something from their anorak and we left nibbling on smoke hardened meats. The honey on my salmon flakes seemed to lighten my feet. I sucked on it in my cheek like my Father Oaván had taught me.

Several kilometers along the rim of the canyon, Guhtur spotted potholes in the sand stone filled with water. Each was capped with a thin layer of ice. The frosted surface of two of the depressions were fractured and there was plenty of goat sign and tracks near the water.

"Look Father Oaván," Guhtur said, "The troll was here too."

"Boys, keep your eyes open. The goats will be frightened and there is likely more than one troll prowling this area." He licked a finger and held it in the air. "There is no wind which will work to our advantage."

Elnar looked tired sitting next to the water holes in the rocks. "Father Oaván," I pointed at Elnar. "He may need to slow down."

My father knelt and started looking over my friend. Guhtur stood watch on a ledge above us while I aided Father Oaván.

At first, Elnar complained of his feet. Father removed his shoes and discovered a pair of pebble-sized blisters on the back of each heal. But while I helped Father seal these with synthetic skin, Elnar's eyes rolled back into his head and he slumped into the dust.

Father Oaván lifted his head and checked his facemask. Its filters were caked with dust and fines, and the reserve air tank was running dangerously low. I searched through Elnar's ruck, but only found his pad and some packaged energy nuggets.

Frustrated with my friend's naiveté, I removed my spare canister and plugged it into his mask while Father brushed as much dirt out of the filters as he could. Soon enough Elnar woke, but he complained of his head pounding, and began to weep.

"Son," said Father Oaván to me, "now is the time when men must make difficult decisions."

Father Oaván did not need to continue his thought. I could see that Elnar needed to return to the longhouse and he would require help to get there. "Father, I will do the hard thing, because it is the right thing. Let me take Elnar back to the long house. You and Guhtur return to the hunt and find our family a buck."

He smiled at me. "You are a good son, Birki. I am proud of you."

I hefted my ruck and pulled Elnar's arm over my shoulder. Guthur took Elnar's ruck and spear, stuffing the energy nuggets into my bag, before slugging me in the arm. "You're probably going to need these."

With at least twenty kilometers distance between the dwelling, and us we probably would not arrive there until well after the winter twilight fell. I wasted no more time and set off, half-supporting Elnar as he hobbled beside me.

The cleaner filters helped Elnar to breath better. Soon he was walking on his own a couple of paces ahead of me. I tried to encourage him, but he responded with silence. I walked along behind him lost in thought for a while. While glad my father was proud of me, I regretted returning from my first Joulupukki with nothing.

The long needled pines and narrow spruce endemic to the southern reaches of Mars passed, but I remained lost in thought. Suddenly, I heard a loud snort from the dense grove directly ahead. I quickly grabbed Elnar's shoulder and pushed him to the ground. The two of us rolled into the powdery snow and sedges that covered the ground and then scrambled behind the trunk of a spruce.

For their size, peikko were quiet when they moved over the ground. I strained to listen and realized that the beast must have made a kill. It chomped on flesh and bone with indifference. My bowels froze when it paused in its feast to look over its shoulder in our direction, but the boughs of the tree concealed us from its gaze. And the air remained still.

I could see no way around the troll. To our right the sheer canyon wall fell maybe one-hundred meters. On the left thick trees would slow us down if we ran, while the beast could simply plow through them. I checked my reserve gauge. We had some time to wait, but it would be a close thing.

Quietly pulling my pad from my ruck and handing it to Elnar, I whispered into his ear, "Call the hunt. Let them know where we are."

As I rolled over the wind caressing the back of my neck, carrying my sent into the Troll's grove, decided my only course of action. I removed the scabbard from my spearhead and prepared to charge. When the troll lifted its keen nose into the air, I realized that this was the one we had seen below in the canyon earlier that day. It sniffed the air and peered into the trees, leaving the remains of its kill behind for the moment, pawing the dirt with its great roan fists. I sprang from my hiding place.

About the Author

Matthew Alan Thyer is an independent author writing hard-science fiction with a twist. Currently publishing a series of stories which share the theme "sports in space." He is an Army veteran who served as a signals intelligence analyst. Prior to finding his voice as a writer he worked as an operations engineer, wildland firefighter, backcountry ranger, kayak guide and river rat.

Matt's hobbies include trail running, backpacking, skiing, mountaineering, bicycling, and paragliding.

www.ingramcontent.com/pod-product-compliance
Lightning Source LLC
Chambersburg PA
CBHW070644130626
46555CB00006B/2697